THE BAD GUYS' QUOTE BOOK

"An inspiring testament to the vitality and resilience of the human spirit."
—Alexander Cockburn

"A few words from the bosses—and the bosses of bosses. Sound bad advice."
—*Playboy*

DON'T YOU WISH YOU HAD SAID IT?

"Don't get mad, get even."
—Joseph P. Kennedy

"I have spent a lot of time searching through the Bible for loopholes."
—W. C. Fields

"Take no prisoners!"

—General George
Armstrong Custer

THE BAD GUYS' QUOTE BOOK

COMPILED BY
ROBERT SINGER

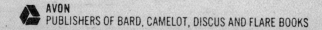
AVON
PUBLISHERS OF BARD, CAMELOT, DISCUS AND FLARE BOOKS

THE BAD GUYS' QUOTE BOOK is an original publication of Avon Books. This work has never before appeared in book form.

AVON BOOKS
A division of
The Hearst Corporation
1790 Broadway
New York, New York 10019

First Avon Printing, July, 1984

AVON TRADEMARK REG. U.S. PAT. OFF. AND IN
OTHER COUNTRIES, MARCA REGISTRADA, HECHO EN
U. S. A.

Printed in the U. S. A.

WFH 10 9 8 7 6 5 4 3 2 1

For
Thomas King Forcade
1945–1978

"So I lied. So what?"

Table of Contents

Introduction

The quotations in this book really need no introduction. "Don't get mad, get even"—a great quote by a great guy, Joseph P. Kennedy—is as perfectly lapidary and succinct as anyone could ask. "Don't get mad . . ."—this is all ye know and all ye need to know. . . .

If you would like to think like a Vanderbilt or a Morgan, or know what Al Capone or Arnold Rothstein might have said in certain circumstances (perhaps you find yourself in such circumstances, now and then), this book will tell you how and what. Far be it from the management of *The Bad Guys' Quote Book* to endorse the sentiments expressed herein. For example, I, personally, do not subscribe to points of view as extreme as that of Edward "Spike" O'Donnell ("When arguments fail, use a blackjack"). Yet, because we forget how many people do lean to such a philosophy, it is useful to have Mr. O'Donnell's doctrine filed at our fingertips (themselves filed), in his original phrasing. It is, indeed, all too easy to forget that this old world is filled to about nine-tenths of capacity with gentlemen and ladies who think *exactly* like Mr. O'Donnell, and practice what he preached. With my trusty little book as your *constant* companion, you'll be that much less at a loss for the right wrong words when the need to speak them arises. It may even remind you to, as Jake "The Raging Bull" La-Motta's father told him when he was eight years old, handing the tot an ice pick, "Next time, hit 'em hard and hit 'em first."

—R. Singer

THE BAD GUYS' QUOTE BOOK

Do It!

"Keep patting your enemy on the back until a small bullet hole appears between your fingers."
—Joseph Bonanno

"Other people talk about the overpopulation problem. At least I'm doing something about it."
—accused murderer (Reported from the Tombs by Joe Schenkman, artist.)

"If I made peace with Russia today, I'd only attack her again tomorrow. I just couldn't help myself."
—Adolf Hitler

"Kill for the love of killing! Kill for the love of Kali!"
—Hindu saying

"Show them no mercy if they resist."
—Captain Bligh

"I don't give a shit what happens. I want you all to stonewall it. Let them plead the Fifth Amendment, cover up, or anything else if it'll save the plan."
—Richard Nixon

"Grab 'em by the nose and kick 'em in the pants!"
—General George Patton

13

"When you pull a gun, kill a man."
> —Walter Brennan, in *My Darling Clementine* (screenplay by Samuel G. Engel and Winston Miller)

"Go out and tell a lie that will make the whole family proud of you."
> —Cadmus, to Pentheus, in *The Bacchae* by Euripides (453 B.C.)

"When arguments fail, use a blackjack!"
> —Edward "Spike" O'Donnell, Al Capone associate

"Always run from a knife and rush a gun."
> —Jimmy Hoffa

"Rule the Empire through force."
> —Shogun Tokugawa

"Steal this book."
> —Abbie Hoffman

"Kill your parents."
> —Jerry Rubin

"Do what thou wilt shall be the whole of the Law."
> —Aleister Crowley

"You better do the right thing."
> —Jimmy "the Weasel" Fratianno

"We will do anything to keep this company alive."
> —John DeLorean

"Let's do it."

—Gary Gilmore, to his firing squad

"I Did It My Way."

—Sid Vicious, of the Sex Pistols

Don't Do It!

"Don't go broke, go public."
>—Wall Street wisdom

"Don't get mad, get even."
>—Joseph P. Kennedy

"Don't get mad, get interest."
>—The Unknown Coke Dealer

"You do not lament the loss of hair of one who has been beheaded."
>—Joseph Stalin

"Don't steal the hubcaps. Steal the car."
>—Frank Sinatra

"My philosophy is: Don't think."
>—Charles Manson

"You don't need to be ordering fancy duds. You're going to prison. Why don't you have a suit made with stripes on it?"
>—Al Capone's bodyguard, to his boss while at the tailor's

"It is impossible to obtain a conviction for sodomy from an English jury. Half of them don't believe that it can physically be done, and the other half are doing it."

—Winston Churchill

"Don't get the idea that I'm one of those goddamn radicals. Don't get the idea that I'm knocking the American system."

—Al Capone

"Never hit a prisoner over the head with your pistol, because you may afterwards want to use your weapon and find it disabled."

—General D. J. Cook, Superintendent of the Rocky Mountain Detective Association

"Don't forget to split all my infinitives."

—Dutch Schultz, to reporters at a press conference

"Don't say yes until I finish talking."

—Darryl F. Zanuck

"If you don't say anything, you won't be called on to repeat it."

—Calvin Coolidge

"When you say that you agree to a thing in principle, you mean that you have not the slightest intention of carrying it out in practice."

—Otto von Bismarck

"Never trust an automatic pistol or a D.A.'s deal."

—John Dillinger

"Just because I turn down a contract on a guy doesn't mean he isn't going to get hit."
                    —"Joey," hit man

"Thank God I've always avoided persecuting my enemies."
                    —Adolf Hitler

Why'dja Do It?

"I wrecked trains because I like to see people die. I like to hear them scream."

> —Sylvestre Matuschka, "the Hungarian Train Wreck Freak" (Escaped prison 1937, not heard from since.)

"I never killed a man who didn't need it."
> —Clay Allison, Old West outlaw

"I never killed a man that didn't deserve it."
> —Mickey Cohen

"I acted to show my love for Jodie Foster."
> —John Hinckley

"The only two things that motivate me and that matter to me are revenge and guilt."
> —Elvis Costello

"I never cheated an honest man, only rascals. They wanted something for nothing. I gave them nothing for something."
> —Joseph "Yellow Kid" Weil, con man

"I just wanted to see what it looked like in the spotlight."
> —Jim Morrison

"We were driven to it."
                    —Jesse James

"That feeling just came over me."
                    —Albert DeSalvo, the Boston
                    Strangler

"I truly wish I could be a great surgeon or philoso-
pher or author or anything constructive, but in all
honesty I'd rather turn up my amplifier full blast
and drown myself in the noise."
                    —Charles Schmid, "the Tuc-
                    son Murderer"

"That's where the money was."
                    —Willie Sutton, on being asked
                    why he robbed a bank

"You can imagine my embarrassment when I
killed the wrong guy."
                    —Joe Valachi

"I like to crush their egos."
                    —Bobby Fischer, age 10,
                    chess master

"I wanted to make it an even fifty."
                    —Monk Eastman

"I did it for the money."
                    —Alfred Krupp, German in-
                    dustrialist under Hitler

"I was only following orders."
                    —Adolf Eichmann

"I was only giving orders."
                    —Thomas King Forcade, pub-
                    lisher, *High Times*

"Nobody's perfect."
                    —Joe E. Lewis

"I'm sorry I missed."
                    —Squeaky Fromme

Roots

"For sheets my mother used to sew together old cement bags."
                    —Joe Valachi

"When I was eight years old I came home with tears in my eyes because some kids had stolen my samwich. My father handed me an ice pick, and said, 'Next time, hit 'em first and hit 'em hard.' "
                    —Jake LaMotta

"If I had not been born Perón, I would have liked to be Perón."
                    —Juan Perón

"Where I come from, we don't get fucked without getting kissed."
                    —Jimmy "the Weasel" Fratianno

"I am a member of the rabble in good standing."
                    —Westbrook Pegler

"I was a woman at six."
                    —Jill St. John

"I went to my mother and told her I intended to commence a different life. I asked for and obtained her blessing and at once I commenced the career of a robber."
                    —Tiburcio Vasquez, California outlaw

"I suppose there are two things I miss: I often think it would have been nice to have had a mother when I was a little boy, and, yes, sometimes I think it would be quite nice to be considered a good guy."

>—Allen Klein, former lawyer for the Beatles and the Rolling Stones

"I was born in a barrel of butcher knives
Trouble I love and peace I despise
Wild horses kicked me in my side
Then a rattlesnake bit me and he walked off and
    died."

>—Bo Diddley

"My father was a saint, I'm not."

>—Indira Gandhi

"I did not look behind me, 'till I got to St. Omer's & thence fled to America; here I offer'd to become a Spy for the English Government which was scornfully rejected; I then turned to Plunder & Libel the Yankees, for which I was Fined 5000 Dollars & kicked out of the Country! I came back to England (after absconding for Seven years) & set up the Crown & Mitre to establish my Loyalty!—accepted from the Doctor £400 to print & disperse a pamphlet against 'the Hellfire of Reform' . . . but applied the Money to purchase an estate at Botley, & left ye Doctor to pay the Paper & Printing! Being now Lord of the Manor, I began by sowing the seeds of discontent through Hampshire: I oppressed the Poor, sent the Aged to Hell, & damned the eyes of my Parish Apprentices before they were open'd in the morning! . . . and being now supported by a Band of Reformers, I renewed my old favorite Toast of Damnation to the House of Brunswick! & being exalted by the sale of 10,000 Political Registers every week, I find myself the greatest Man in the World! except that Idol of all my Adorations, his Royal & Imperial Majesty, NAPOLEONE!"

—William Cobbett, British journalist

The Big Time

"I can hire one half of the working class to kill the other half."
>—Jay Gould

"We should keep the Panama Canal. After all, we stole it fair and square."
>—S. I. Hayakawa

"We'll blast them back to the Stone Age."
>—General William Westmoreland, U.S. commander in Vietnam

"It was necessary to destroy the town in order to save it."
>—The Pentagon Papers

"Easy. I own Chicago. I own Miami. I own Las Vegas."
>—Sam Giancana, when asked what he did for a living

"We're bigger than U. S. Steel."
>—Meyer Lansky, on organized crime

"L'état c'est moi." (The state, that's me.)
>—Louis XIV

"Money talks. The more money, the louder it talks."

—Arnold Rothstein

"Anybody has a right to evade taxes if he can get away with it. No citizen has a moral obligation to assist in maintaining his government."

—J. P. Morgan

"Inventory in Action"

—slogan of the American Express Field Warehousing Corporation, found liable in 1963 for loans made against its bonds on $175-million worth of nonexistent salad oil in Bayonne, New Jersey

"The public be damned! I'm working for my stockholders."

—William Henry Vanderbilt

"I've got Hubert's pecker in my pocket."

—Lyndon B. Johnson

"Another improvement . . . was that we built our gas chambers to accommodate two thousand people at one time."

—Rudolf Hess

"What do I care about the law? Ain't I got the power?"

—Cornelius Vanderbilt

"I'm in charge here."

—Alexander Haig

"You show me how to put two million dollars in a suitcase and I'll give you the two million dollars."
—Frank Sinatra

"The illegal we do immediately. The unconstitutional takes a bit longer."
—Henry Kissinger

"Don't see 'em this big out here, do they?"
—Lyndon B. Johnson, exposing himself to reporters in a public toilet during a tour of the Far East

"A billion here, a billion there—pretty soon you're talking about real money."
—Senator Everett Dirksen, on the U.S. defense budget

What's the Diff?

"The people of Zaire are not thieves. It merely happens that they move things or borrow them."
—President Mobutu Sese Seko

"If one offers money to a government to influence it, that is corruption. But if someone receives money for services rendered afterward, that is a commission."
—Adnan Khashoggi, Saudi arms dealer

"I was offered a job as a hoodlum and I turned it down cold. A thief is anybody who gets out and works for his living, like robbing a bank or breaking into a place and stealing stuff, or kidnapping somebody. He really gives some effort to it. A hoodlum is a pretty lousy sort of scum. He works for gangsters and bumps guys off when they have been put on the spot. Why, after I'd made my rep, some of the Chicago Syndicate wanted me to work for them as a hood—you know, handling a machine gun. They offered me two hundred and fifty dollars a week and all the protection I needed. I was on the lam at the time and not able to work at my regular line. But I wouldn't consider it. 'I'm a thief,' I said. 'I'm no lousy hoodlum.' "
—Alvin Karpis, "Public Enemy Number One"

"Cocaine isn't habit forming. I should know—I've been using it for years."
                    —Tallulah Bankhead

"Trust is good, but control is better."
                    —Feliks Dzerzhinski, founder
                    of Soviet Cheka, now the KGB

"We're going to move left and right at the same time."
                    —Jerry Brown

" 'The Beast' [Al Capone] uses his musclemen to peddle rotgut alcohol and green beer. I'm a legitimate salesman of good beer and pure whiskey. He trusts nobody and suspects everybody. He always has guards. I travel around with a couple of pals. 'The Behemoth' can't sleep nights. If you ask me, he's on dope. Me, I don't even need an aspirin."
                    —George "Bugs" Moran

"When I sell liquor, it's called bootlegging; when my patrons serve it on silver trays on Lake Shore Drive, it's called hospitality."
                    —Al Capone

"I'm not against the police; I'm just afraid of them."
                    —Alfred Hitchcock

"I love treason but hate a traitor."
                    —Julius Caesar

"He [Julius Caesar] was a husband to every wife and a wife to every husband."
                    —Suetonius

"In Italy for thirty years under the Borgias they had warfare, terror, murder, bloodshed, but they produced Michaelangelo, Leonardo da Vinci and the Renaissance. In Switzerland, they had brotherly love, they had five hundred years of democracy and peace. And what did they produce? The cuckoo-clock."

—Orson Welles

"An honest politician is one who when he is bought will stay bought."

—Simon Camerson, British political commentator

"When the President does it, that means it is not illegal."

—Richard Nixon

"I don't like the Dutchman. He's a crocodile. He's sneaky. I don't trust him."

—Jack "Legs" Diamond, just before a peace conference with Dutch Schultz

"I don't trust Legs. He's nuts. He gets excited and starts pulling a trigger like another guy wipes his nose."

—Dutch Schultz, just before a peace conference with "Legs" Diamond

"Only two kinds of witnesses exist. The first live in a neighborhood where a crime has been committed and in no circumstances have ever seen anything or even heard a shot. The second category are the neighbors of anyone who happens to be accused of the crime. These have always looked out of their windows when the shot was fired, and have noticed the accused person standing peaceably on his balcony a few yards away."

—Sicilian police officer

"Mao's poems are better than Hitler's paintings but not as good as Winston Churchill's."

—Arthur Waley, scholar of the Far East

Amore

"In the sex field, you can be totally stupid and still make money."
— Al Goldstein, editor of *Screw*

"Apparently, the way to a girl's heart is to saw her in half."
— Victor Mature

"With women, I've got a long bamboo pole with a leather loop on the end of it. I slip the loop around their necks so they can't get away or come too close. Like catching snakes."
— Marlon Brando

"I promise every German girl a husband."
— Adolf Hitler

"Paranoia is just a kind of awareness, and awareness is just a form of love."
— Charles Manson

"I wasn't going to rob her, or touch her, or rape her. I just wanted to kill her."
— David Berkowitz

"I have often looked at women and committed adultery in my heart."
— Jimmy Carter

"A woman who is unfaithful deserves to be shot."

—Pancho Villa

Who, Me?

"**M**y word, gentlemen, when you come to know me better you'll see how utterly ridiculous it is for a man like me to be in the clutches of the law. Why, I've never even been given a ticket for speeding."
>—Henry Judd Gray, murderer

"Raaly, this is a surprise. You quite have the advantage of me, don't you know. I raaly cawn't say that I evah saw you befoah. My name is James Wilfred Adair."
>—Nicky Arnstein, con man

"I am John Schwartz, who is Alfred Packer?"
>—Alfred Packer, cannibal

"I admit I'm a gambler."
>—Vincent Ciucci, charged with murdering his wife and three children

"I'm sorry it happened, it was just a piece of hotheaded foolishness."
>—Dion O'Bannion, on a 1920's rub-out

"If you guys have a beef with her, that's her problem. Don't lay it on me. The old lady has to take care of her own weight."

> —Herbie Sperling, convicted heroin dealer, on being arrested for narcotics possession at his mother's house

"Damned if I know. And you can be fuckin' sure I'll never rent no car from Avis again."

> —Herbie Sperling, on the meaning of two pistols and an axe used in three murders being found in the trunk of his rented car

"I'm just an old retired investor, living on a pension."

> —Meyer Lansky

Let's Make a Deal!

"**I**f you want to take my picture, it'll cost you a fiver. If not, I'll smash your camera."
— Sid Vicious

"Public service is my motto."
— Al Capone

"I never did anything to deserve that reputation unless it was to supply good beer to people who wanted it."

— Dutch Schultz, on being designated Public Enemy Number One

"You can't get anything without paying for it."
— Boss Tweed

"Hey Sam, how about a loan?"
"Whattaya need?"
"Oh, about $500."
"Whattaya got for collateral?"
"Whattaya need?"
"How about an eye?"

— Sam Giancana, small talk

"Don't buy a landslide. I don't want to pay for one more vote than I have to."

— Joseph P. Kennedy on JFK's election strategy

For a Few Dollars More

"I've realized, after fourteen months in this country, the value of money, whether it is clean or dirty."

—Nguyen Cao Ky

"Always overpay your income taxes. That way, you'll get a refund."

—Meyer Lansky

"When I first met Elvis, he had a million dollars' worth of talent. Today he has a million dollars."

—Colonel Tom Parker

"I shall consider it my patriotic duty to keep Elvis in the ninety per cent bracket."

—Colonel Tom Parker

"I steal."

—Sam Giancana, explaining his livelihood to his draft board

"I find this corpse guilty of carrying a concealed weapon and I fine it $40."

—Judge Roy Bean, finding a pistol and $40 on a man he'd just shot

"A verbal contract isn't worth the paper it's written on."

—Samuel Goldwyn

"The capitalists will sell us the length of rope with which we will destroy them."
                    —Lenin

"I would gladly pay you Tuesday for a hamburger today."
                    —J. Wellington Wimpy

"You like federal judges? I'll buy you one for Christmas."
                    —Joey Gallo

"The cost of living has just gone up another dollar a quart."
                    —W. C. Fields

"We want to clean out the pigsty, get rid of the pigs, and get our own snouts into the trough."
                    —Ernst Rohm, storm trooper

"Whatever is not nailed down is mine. Whatever I can pry up is not nailed down."
                    —Collis P. Huntington, railroad
                    tycoon

Tricks of the Trade

"The best way to make money is to make money."

—old counterfeiters' saying

"He tried to steal more chain than he could swim with."

—old slave traders' joke

"How much do you want it to be?"

—old accountants' riddle (answering the question, How much is 2 + 2?)

"It's crackers to slip the rozzer the dropsy in snide." (It's crazy to pay off the police in counterfeit money.)

—Cockney business motto

"Both liars and the incurably shy can convince others of their sincerity by looking not into a person's eyes but at the space between them."

—Neville Gerson

No More Mr. Nice Guy

"If it takes a bloodbath, let's get it over with."
　　　　　　—Ronald Reagan

"If any demonstrator ever lays down in front of my car, it'll be the last car he ever lays down in front of."
　　　　　　—George Wallace

"I shall come to you in the night and we shall see who is stronger—a little girl who won't eat her dinner or a great big man with cocaine in his veins."
　　　　　　—Sigmund Freud, to his fiancée

"We will bury you."
　　　　　　—Nikita Khrushchev

"The greatest joy a man can know is to conquer his enemies and drive them before him. To ride their horses and take away their possessions. To see the faces of those who were dear to them bedewed with tears, and to clasp their wives and daughters to his arms."
　　　　　　—Genghis Khan

"Winning isn't everything. It's the only thing."
　　　　　　—Vince Lombardi

"This won't be the first time I've arrested some-body and then built my case afterward."
>   —New Orleans District Attor-ney Jim Garrison

"You make the spitballs and I'll throw them."
>   —Nelson Rockefeller

"If you start throwing hedgehogs under me, I shall throw two porcupines under you."
>   —Nikita Khrushchev

"Cut a man's hand when you fight him. He'll freeze, fascinated by the sight of his own blood. That's when you stick him in the throat."
>   —Gerry Youghkins, cutlery expert

"If I had time to clear up the mess, I'd shoot you."
>   —J. R. Ewing

"This is for you, Frank."
>   —Frank "The Chin" Gigante, as he shot Frank Costello in the head

"I'm going to shoot some pheasants."
>   —Sam "Golf Bag" Hunt, ex-plaining to a policeman why he was carrying a shotgun in a golf bag

"Take that, you dirty son of a bitch."
>   —Mike Genna's dying words as he kicked a stretcher bear-er in the face

"I challenge the murderers of Dion O'Bannion to shoot it out with me at State and Madison!"
                    —Louis "Three Gun" Alterie

"You've reached a ripe old age."
                    —Louis "Lepke" Buchalter

"Damn your eyes for a parcel of lubberly rascals."
                    —Captain Bligh

"You can't go into the ring and be a nice guy. I would go a month, two months, without having sex. It worked for me because it made me a vicious animal. You can't fight if you have any compassion or anything like that."
                    —Jake LaMotta

"It is of no odds to us if we kill someone."
                    —Heinrich Himmler

"There's more than one way to die."
                    —Tony "Big Tuna" Accarda

"If only the Roman people had a single neck!"
                    —Caligula

"I will make you shorter by the head."
                    —Elizabeth I

"We'll scratch your goodies out . . . we'll blow your sillies off."
                    —Yoko Ono

"I'll kill the son of a bitch."
                    —Jack Ruby

"I'll moider da bum."
                    —"Two-Ton" Tony Galento

War and Peace

"Three cheers for war in general!"
—Benito Mussolini

"Thank goodness we don't live in medieval times when people fought wars over ideas."
—General Wojciech Jaruzelski

"One of the problems we're going to have to solve is to make the Armed Forces so popular, everyone wants to get in."
—General Lewis B. Hershey

"And throughout the war we never lost a battle."
—General William Westmoreland, U.S. commander in Vietnam

"No man with gumption wants a woman to fight his nation's battles."
—General William Westmoreland

"I'm going to Vietnam at the request of the White House. President Johnson says a war isn't really a war without my jokes."
—Bob Hope

"I call it the 'Madman Theory.' I want the North Vietnamese to believe that I've reached the point where I might do *anything* to stop the war. We'll just slip the word to them that 'For God's sake, you know, Nixon is obsessed about Communism. We can't restrain him when he's angry—and he has his hand on the nuclear button.' "

—Richard Nixon

"I would say that anything that is indecent and violent in TV is a crime against humanity, and they should shoot the head man responsible."

—Ted Turner, cable-TV network owner

Nice Place

"This is virgin territory for whorehouses."
                    —Al Capone, on suburbia

"A real goddamn crazy place! Nobody's safe in
the streets!"
                    —Lucky Luciano, on Chicago

"If you think the United States has stood still,
who built the largest shopping center in the
world?"
                    —Richard Nixon

"GO AWAY"
                    —Inscription on the doormat
                    at the home of Sam Giancana

"This establishment goes unconditionally with
the Führer."
                    —slogan of Wittenau lunatic
                    asylum

"If you smell gunpowder you're in Cicero."
                    —Chicago wag

"If built in great numbers, motels will be used for
nothing but illegal purposes."
                    —J. Edgar Hoover

"NO OPIUM-SMOKING IN THE ELEVATORS"
>—sign, Rand Hotel, New York, 1907

"If England treats her criminals the way she has treated me, she doesn't deserve to have any."
>—Oscar Wilde

"While we are sleeping, two-thirds of the world are plotting to do us in."
>—Dean Rusk

"I want my own fucking country."
>—Robert Vesco

"The Germans are always either at your feet or at your throat."
>—Winston Churchill

"Jersey City is the moralest [sic] city in America."
>—former mayor Frank Hague

"TRESPASSERS WILL BE EATEN"
>—sign on the gate of a lion-guarded estate of Ken Burnstine, marijuana smuggler

"This was a wonderful prison. I recommend it as a vacation spot."
>—"Dapper Dan" Collins, con man

Great Advice

"I knew one thing: as soon as anyone said you didn't need a gun, you'd better take one along that worked."

—Raymond Chandler

"You must put the worm on the hook before the fish will bite."

—Reverend Jim Jones

"Better tried by twelve than carried by six."

—Jeff Cooper

"Never steal more than you actually need, for the possession of surplus money leads to extravagance, foppish attire, frivolous thought."

—Dalton Trumbo

"Fuck ethics."

—Michelangelo Antonioni

"The first duty of a revolutionary is to get away with it."

—Abbie Hoffman

"Live fast, die young, and have a good-looking corpse."

—Willard Motley

"I think any man in business would be foolish to fool around with his secretary. If it's somebody else's secretary, fine."

—Barry Goldwater

"Buy gold, silver, Swiss francs and a gun."

—Harry Browne, investment adviser

"When you lose your money you lose nothing. When you lose your soul you lose everything."

—Meyer Lansky

"The best ways are the most straightforward ways. When you're sitting around scamming these things out, all kinds of James Bondian ideas come forth, but when it gets down to the reality of it, the simplest and most straightforward way is usually the best, and the way that attracts the least attention. Also, pouring gasoline on the water and lighting it like James Bond doesn't work either. . . . They tried it during Prohibition."

—Thomas King Forcade, marijuana smuggler

"*Mundus vult decipi decipiatur ergo.* The world wants to be cheated, so cheat."

—Xaviera Hollander

"If you look rather casual with the knife when you flick it open, people don't like it."

>—Gerry Youghkins, cutlery
>expert

The Pause that Refreshes

"Would you please have another look at my nose and put in that cocaine stuff. . . ."
>—Adolf Hitler (Quoted by Dr. Giesing in Nuremberg trial testimony, 1947.)

"This stuff is as good as gold."
>—John DeLorean

"But when you sniff cocaine it gets into your clothes, down your neck, under your nails."
>—Caresse Crosby, jazz-age flapper

"I've never had a problem with drugs; I've had problems with the police."
>—Keith Richards

"I never turned blue in anyone's bathroom. I think that's the height of bad taste."
>—Keith Richards

Quer, Introspection 3

Quiet Introspection

"The populace may hiss at me, but when I go home and think of my money, I applaud myself."
> —Horace

"I should have put the bum away early, but my timing was a fraction of an iota off."
> —Philadelphia Jack O'Brian, pugilist

"I always thought I was Jeanne d'Arc and Bonaparte. How little one knows oneself."
> —Charles de Gaulle, on being compared to Robespierre

"I'd rather have a free bottle in front of me than a pre-frontal lobotomy."
> —S. Clay Wilson, artist

"I am in the habit of shooting from time to time, and if I sometimes make mistakes, at least I have shot."
> —Hermann Göring

"Yeah, sure, now beat it."
> —Sam Giancana, to an evangelist who asked if he was a Christian

"One night, nobody was paying any attention to me, so I thought I'd commit suicide. So I went in the bathroom, broke a glass and slashed my chest with it. It's a really good way to get attention. I'm going to do it again, particularly as it doesn't work."

—Sid Vicious

"I wear a Nazi uniform to show I'm anti-Nazi."
—Brian Jones

"I have been too lenient."
—Adolf Hitler

"I didn't inherit any money."
—Moe Dalitz

"I consider that day misspent that I am not either charged with a crime, or arrested for one."
—"Ratsy" Tourbillon

"I've been shot and missed so often I've a notion to hire out as a professional target. Life with me is just one bullet after another."
—Edward "Spike" O'Donnell

"I have no desire whatever to reform myself. My only desire is to reform people who try to reform me. And I believe that the only way to reform people is to kill 'em."
—Carl Panzram, mass murderer

"You dare to question my orders?"
—Captain Bligh

"There's no justice in this world."

       —Frank Costello, on the prosecution of Lucky Luciano by District Attorney Thomas Dewey after Luciano had saved Dewey from assassination by Dutch Schultz (by ordering the assassination of Schultz instead)

See?

"You see that fucking fish? If he'd kept his mouth shut he wouldn'ta got caught."

> —Sam Giancana, on a stuffed swordfish

"When we arrived at the prison gate I looked up and read in large letters over the entrance: 'THE WAY OF THE TRANSGRESSOR IS HARD. ADMISSION, TWENTY-FIVE CENTS' but I was on the dead-head list and went in free."

> —Johnny Reno, Old West gun-slinger

"I saw a closed car speeding away with what looked like a telephone receiver sticking out the rear window spitting fire."

> —Mrs. Bach, witness to a Chicago shootout

"You know, I go live out in the desert and I see a lot of madness. I see big fat people coming around with guns, shooting lizards, spiders, birds, anything they can get their hands on. They're all programmed to kill."

> —Charles Manson

"I see many enemies around and mighty few friends."

> —Billy the Kid

65

"If you've seen one city slum, you've seen them all."

> —Spiro T. Agnew

"I'll pull your eyeballs out."

> —Dyno DeStefano, Chicago bill collector

"You recognize a federal agent, you find any here, you tell me. I'll have him locked up and he won't be turned loose till you say so."

> —"Papa Doc" Duvalier, to Vincent Teresa

"The first guy that rats gets a bellyful of slugs in the head. Understand?"

> —Joey Glimco, trade unionist

"Enjoy the view?"

> —Captain Bligh to a man who froze in a block of ice while being punished by posting in the crow's nest of the H.M.S. *Bounty* as it rounded the Cape of Good Hope

Do Unto Others

"**I** can't stand squealers. Hit that guy."
>—Albert Anastasia

"Who will free me from this turbulent priest?"
>—Henry II, "ordering" the murder of Saint Thomas à Becket

"The time to kill a snake is when you've got the hoe in your hands."
>—Lyndon B. Johnson

"He is crazy; if he comes back shoot him on sight."
>—Adolf Hitler, on Rudolf Hess

"*Carthago delenda est.*" (Carthage must be destroyed.)
>—Cicero

"*Hanoi delenda est.*"
>—P. J. O'Rourke

"Hit him on the head!"
>—Boris Badenov

"Let them eat cake."
>—Marie Antoinette

"I ate them before they ate me."
>—Idi Amin Dada

"Life in this society being, at best, an utter bore and no aspect of society being at all relevant to women, there remains to civic-minded responsible, thrill-seeking females only to overthrow the government, eliminate the money system, institute complete automation and destroy the male sex."

—Valerie Solanas, radical feminist

"Pope Leo used to cite his father, Lorenzo de' Medici, who often said, 'Remember that those who speak ill of us don't love us.'"

—Francesco Guicciardini

"Enemy—SP (Suppressive Person) Order. Fair Game. May be deprived of property or injured by any means by any Scientologist without any discipline of the Scientologist. May be tricked, sued or lied to or destroyed."

—L. Ron Hubbard, "Fair Game Doctrine"

"Take him for a ride."

—Hymie Weiss

"If you give me six lines written by the most honest man, I will find something in them to hang him."

—Cardinal Richelieu

"I may not have shot anyone yet, but I always travel around with a little list of people who might be suitable for assassination one day."

—Auberon Waugh

"As some day it may happen that a victim must
    be found
I've got a little list—I've got a little list
Of society offenders who might well be under-
    ground
And who never would be missed—who never
    would be missed."
                        —W. S. Gilbert

   "Let him turn and twist slowly, slowly in the
wind."
                        —John Ehrlichman

Numero Uno

"I myself consider myself the most powerful figure in the world."
>   —Idi Amin Dada

"I'm Tommy O'Connor and I've just escaped from the county jail! Drive like hell!"
>   —"Terrible" Tommy O'Connor

"I am the devil and I have come to do the devil's work!"
>   —Charles "Tex" Watson, Charles Manson associate

"I am deeply hurt by your calling me a woman hater. But I am a monster. I am the Son of Sam."
>   —David Berkowitz

"I am not a crook."
>   —Richard Nixon

"I'm not a bad guy. I'm just like everybody else."
>   —Sonny Liston

"I want to get killed in one hell-firing minute of smoking action."
>   —"Blackface" Charley Bryant, Dalton gang member

"I am what you call a hooligan!"
>   —Emmeline Pankhurst, British suffragette

"I want to go out in a blaze of glory."
>   —David Berkowitz

"I want peace and I will live and let live."
>   —Al Capone

"From now on, Sidney, you can just call the five of us the barbershop quintet."
>   —"Crazy Joe" Gallo, after the murder of Albert Anastasia by five men in a barbershop

"I'm no peace creep in any sense of the word."
>   —Sonny Barger, President, Hell's Angels M. C.

"For Heaven's sake catch me before I kill more. I cannot help myself."
>   —William Heirens, mass murderer

"I am a deep-dyed scoundrel. But so help me God I was driven to it by oppression and wrong!"
>   —Joaquin Murieta, Old West gunslinger

"I decide. I do. Me."
>   —Frank Hague, former mayor of Jersey City, New Jersey

"I don't have ulcers. I give 'em!"
>   —Lyndon B. Johnson

"No copper will ever take me alive."
                    —George "Machine Gun" Kelly

"I refuse to answer that question on the ground that my answer may tend to degrade or incriminate me."
                    —Arnold Rothstein, gambler

"I don't meet competition. I crush it."
                    —Charles Revson

"Excuse me, I got to go belt somebody."
                    —Humphrey Bogart

"Whatever I do will depend on whether or not it will help me get the nomination."
                    —George Bush

"I trust no one, not even myself."
                    —Joseph Stalin

"My friends call me Ben, Everybody else calls me Mr. Siegel. Why not? That's my name, ain't it?"
                    —Bugsy Siegel

Forgive Me, Father, for I Have Sinned

"God gave me money."
                    —John D. Rockefeller

"If God is one, what is bad?"
                    —Charles Manson

"I have spent a lot of time searching through the Bible for loopholes."
                    —W. C. Fields

"Paris is well worth a mass."
                    —Henri IV

"When somebody protested at [Pope Alexander VI's] wholesale distribution of pardons for the most heinous crimes—one of which included the murder of a daughter by the father—he retorted easily, 'It is not God's will that a sinner should die, but that he should live—and pay.'"
                    —E. R. Chamberlin, *The Bad Popes*

"Judas sold Christ for 30 denari, this man [Pope Alexander VI] would sell him for 29."
                    —Ottaviano Ubaldini, chamberlain to Pope Alexander VI

"God help you if you don't."
>   —Arnold Rothstein, to his bail-
>   bond clients, on the necessity
>   of appearing in court

So Help Me!

"**A**ccording to my best recollection I don't remember."
> —Vincent "Jimmy Blue Eyes"
> Alo

"The little I know, I owe to my ignorance."
> —Sacha Guitry, French playwright

"I have definitional problems with the word 'violence.' I don't know what the word 'violence' means."
> —CIA Director William Colby

"If you don't know what I'm talking about, I share your lack of knowledge. I don't know what I'm talking about."
> —General Lewis B. Hershey

"Boys, I may not know much, but I know the difference between chicken shit and chicken salad."
> —Lyndon B. Johnson

"Baby, let me say this. I got one eye, and that one eye sees a lot of things that my brain tells me I shouldn't talk about. Because my brain says that, if I do, my one eye might not be seeing anything after a while."
> —Sammy Davis, Jr., when asked about Sam Giancana

"Nobody shot me."

> —last words of Frank Gusenberg when asked by police who shot him fourteen times with a machine gun in the Saint Valentine's Day Massacre

"At his sentencing, Herbie Sperling proved that he was the all-time stand-up guy.

"Sperling's lawyer made a lengthy, impassioned plea for his client. He talked of mercy, justice, humanity to fellow men who have chosen the wrong path. Yes, the crimes were serious, yes, Mr. Sperling deserves a prison sentence, but the maximum sentence is not warranted.

"Then the judge turned to Sperling.

" 'Mr. Sperling, is there anything you wish to say?'

" 'Yes, Your Honor. If you think I'm going to beg for mercy, you've got another think coming. You're all a bunch of fucking fascist cocksuckers, you can all go to hell, fuck you, fuck you, fuck you . . .' "

> —Gregory Wallance, *Papa's Game*, a reporter's account of the theft of $72-million worth of confiscated heroin from police custody

"Judge Clark then made a few remarks that I don't now remember, but I do remember that he sentenced me to hard labor in the Missouri Penitentiary for the term of forty years."

> —Johnny Reno, Old West gunslinger

"He didn't know the right people. That's all a police record means."
—Raymond Chandler

"I don't even know what street Canada is on."
—Al Capone

" 'Shut up,' he explained."
—Ring Lardner

Friends in High Places

"**L**iberals are the first to dump you if you con them or get into trouble. Conservatives are better. They never run out on you."
—"Crazy Joe" Gallo

"When I want to buy up any politicians, I always find the anti-monopolists the most purchasable. They don't come so high."
—William Henry Vanderbilt

"Sure there are dishonest men in local government. But there are dishonest men in national government too."
—Richard Nixon

"There is just one thing I can promise you about the outer-space program: your dollars will go farther."
—Wernher von Braun

"The party permits ordinary people to get ahead. Without the party, I couldn't be a mayor."
—Richard Daley, former mayor of Chicago

"Political power grows out of the barrel of a gun."
—Mao Zedong

"Claim everything, concede nothing, and if defeated, allege fraud."

—Tammany Hall maxim

"Tammany, Tammany,
Swamp 'em, swamp 'em,
Get the wampum,
Tam-man-nee!"

—Tammany Hall anthem

"The problem with me is that I am fifty or one hundred years ahead of my time. My speed is very fast. Some ministers have had to drop out of my government because they could not keep up."

—Idi Amin Dada

"I become the problem instead of the solution to the problem."

—Nelson Rockefeller

"I'm 1,000 percent behind Tom Eagleton and I have no intention of dropping him from the ticket."

—George McGovern

"I have no time to prepare a profound message."

—Spiro T. Agnew

"Mankind is tired of liberty."

—Benito Mussolini

"It would take the romance out of old age."

—Frank Hague, former mayor
of Jersey City, New Jersey,
opposing social security legislation

"Nothing would please the Kremlin more than to have the people of this country choose a second-rate President."

—Richard Nixon

"A cardinal rule of politics—never get caught in bed with a live man or a dead woman."

—J. R. Ewing, of *Dallas*

"The first essential for a Prime Minister is to be a good butcher."

—William Ewart Gladstone

"One way to make sure crime doesn't pay would be to let the government run it."

—Ronald Reagan

"My rackets are run on strictly American lines and they're going to stay that way."

—Al Capone

"Vote early and vote often."

—Al Capone (slogan for Big Bill Thompson's anti-reform campaign for Mayor of Chicago, 1926) (Big Bill won.)

Who Done It?

"There's a lot of things blamed on me that never happened. But then, there's a lot of things that I did and never got caught at."
—Johnny Cash

"If everything they say I've done was true, I'd be in a penitentiary long ago."
—Jerry Lee Lewis

"Damn, what made them do that?"
—gambler, commenting on a throw of loaded dice adversely affected by an A-bomb test at Yucca Flat, 75 miles away from Las Vegas

"Only Capone kills like that."
—George "Bugs" Moran, on the Saint Valentine's Day Massacre

"The only man who kills like that is Bugs Moran."
—Al Capone, on the Saint Valentine's Day Massacre

Whatever Gets You Through the Night

"I get sexual satisfaction out of breaking into a place. I don't take anything."

> —William Heirens, convincted burglar, kidnapper, and murderer

"What a thrill that will be if I have to die in the electric chair. It will be the supreme thrill, the only one I haven't tried."

> —Albert Fish, cannibal

"It's a rather pleasant experience to be alone in a bank at night."

> —Willie Sutton

"Once, he [New York Special Prosecutor Maurice Nadjari] compared the thrill of hearing a jury return a guilty verdict to the ultimate sexual experience."

> —Gregory Wallance (Nadjari lost his position due to his failure to obtain convictions.)

"Walking to an appointment with my *masseuse* in Soho this afternoon, I see a group of 'workmen' on a building site and decide to throw some orange peel at them which I always keep in my overcoat pocket for this purpose."

—Auberon Waugh, *Diary*

"I dropped an aerial torpedo right in the center, and the group opened up like a flowering rose. It was most entertaining."

—Vittorio Mussolini

"I can manifest my neurotical emotions, emancipate an epicureal instinct, and elaborate on my heterosexual tendencies."

—Charles Schmid, "the Tucson Murderer"

"If you guys want a sensation, try hauling a corpse around in a car with the hoot owls hooting at you."

—Ralph Jerome von Braun Selz, "The Laughing Murderer"

"I do like to see the arms and legs fly."

—George S. Patton III

"My idea of a wild party is where you throw the girls' panties at the wall and they *stick*."

—Johnny Bob, Native American author

"Nothing in life is so exhilarating as to be shot at without result."

—Winston Churchill

"Do you know the only thing that gives me pleasure? It's to see my dividends coming in."

—John D. Rockefeller

"Goose pimples rose all over me, my hair stood on end, my eyes filled with tears of love and gratitude for this greatest of all conquerors of human misery and shame, and my breath came in little gasps. If I had not known that the Leader would have scorned such adulation, I might have fallen to my knees in unashamed worship, but instead I drew myself to attention, raised my arm in the eternal salute of the ancient Roman Legions and repeated the holy words, 'Heil Hitler!' "

—George Lincoln Rockwell

"I like to dive around in my money like a porpoise and burrow through it like a gopher and toss it up and let it hit me on the head."

—Scrooge McDuck

"All of us should treasure his Oriental wisdom and his preaching of a Zen-like detachment, as exemplified by his constant reminder to clerks, tellers, or others who grew excited by his presence in their banks: 'Just lie down on the floor and keep calm.' "

—Robert Wilson, "John Dillinger Died for You"

"Nothing is so exciting or gathers a crowd so fast as burning a police car."

—Chicago policeman

"Living here in Rio, I have lots of coffees to choose from. And when you're on the lam like me, you appreciate a good cup of coffee."

>   —"Great Train Robber" Ronald Biggs' coffee commercial

"I want a hamburger."

>   —John DeLorean, after posting $10-million bail

"Everything I like is either illegal, immoral or fattening."

>   —Alexander Woollcott

How It Is

"Many a bum show has been saved by the flag."
—George M. Cohan

"The vast majority of women who pretend vaginal orgasm are faking it to 'get the job.' "
—Ti-Grace Atkinson, feminist

"We're big business without high hats."
—Dion O'Bannion

"The only bad publicity is your obituary."
—Douglas Kenney, co-author
of *Animal House*

"It is necessary for me to establish a winner image. Therefore, I have to beat somebody."
—Richard Nixon

"For the Stones, bad news is good news."
—Andrew Oldham ex-manager of the Rolling Stones

"Kissing your hand may make you feel very, very good, but a diamond and sapphire bracelet lasts forever."
—Anita Loos

"Justice is incidental to law and order."
—J. Edgar Hoover

"The race is not always to the swift, nor the battle to the strong—but that's the way to bet."
                    —Damon Runyon

"The cheaper the crook, the gaudier the patter."
                    —Dashiell Hammett

"You can always count on a murderer for a fancy prose style."
                    —Vladimir Nabokov, *Lolita*

"It is ridiculous to call this an industry. This is not. This is rat eat rat, dog eat dog. I'll kill 'em before they kill me. You're talking about the American way of survival of the fittest."
                    —Ray Kroc, chairman of McDonald's

"You want to know how I make my money? There are two million fools born for every intelligent man."
                    —Arnold Rothstein

"Academic freedom can get you killed."
                    —Spiro T. Agnew

"Fortunately the Italian people is not yet accustomed to eating several times per day."
                    —Benito Mussolini

"Without doubt, man is the most dangerous microbe imaginable."
                    —Adolf Hitler

"Too many cooks spoil the brothel."
                    —Polly Adler

"The greatest aid to bigger and better business the criminal has discovered in this generation."

> —*Collier's* magazine description of the Thompson submachine gun

"Nothing is illegal if one hundred businessmen decide to do it."

> —Andrew Young

"A man who has a million dollars is as well off as if he were rich."

> —John Jacob Astor

"The great masses of the people will fall more easily victim to a great lie than to a small one."

> —Adolf Hitler

"They can't get you for what you didn't say."

> —Calvin Coolidge

"Get this straight once and for all. The policeman isn't there to create disorder; he's there to preserve disorder."

> —Richard Daley, former mayor of Chicago

"If a thing's worth having, it's worth cheating for."

> —W. C. Fields

"The criminal is possibly the only human left who looks lovingly on society. He does not hanker to fight it, reform it or even rationalize it. He wants only to rob it."

> —Ben Hecht

My Pal

"[A]nastasio] Somoza may be a son of a bitch, but he's our son of a bitch."
—Franklin D. Roosevelt

"I'm pals with everybody."
—Lucky Luciano

"What's the Constitution between friends?"
—Timothy J. Campbell, to Grover Cleveland, who refused to support an unconstitutional bill

"*Dieu a donc oublié tout ce que j'ai fait pour lui?*" (Has God forgotten everything I've done for him?)
—Louis XIV

"Grant stood by me when I was crazy, and I stood by him when he was drunk, and now we stand by each other."
—General William Sherman

"If Robert Kennedy were alive today, he would support my petition for parole."
—Sirhan Sirhan

"He believed his own publicity. He was called [Sid] Vicious because he was such a wanker. He couldn't fight his way out of a crisp bag."

—Johnny Rotten

"I think he's always nurtured a secret desire to be a hood."

—Bing Crosby, on Frank Sinatra

"Any bootlegger sure is a pal of mine."

—Bessie Smith

"You'd think he'd have the decency to collect my stuff the way I collect him."

—A. J. Weberman, Dylanologist and garbologist, on finding his own writing in Bob Dylan's garbage

"To my dear pal Lucky, from his friend, Frank Sinatra."

—Inscription on a gold cigarette case belonging to Lucky Luciano

"A good housekeeper but a whore at heart."

—Butch Cassidy, on Etta Place

"Hitler had great admiration for Stalin. He was only afraid some radical might come in his place."

—Joachim von Ribbentrop

"I guess he [Harry Truman] will apologize for calling me an s.o.b. and I will apologize for being one."

—John F. Kennedy

"I couldn't have called him an s.o.b. I didn't know he was one at the time."

> —John F. Kennedy, on Canada's Prime Minister John Diefenbaker

"I saw him once in the last twenty years. That was when he shot me."
> —Frank Weiss, talking about his brother Hymie

"We elected our man Nixon president, and if you don't stand behind him, get the hell out of the way so that I can stand behind him."
> —Johnny Cash

"Some of my best friends are MX missiles."
> —Ronald Reagan

"People ask me who my heroes are. I have only one. Hitler. I admire Hitler because he pulled his country together when it was in a terrible state in the early 1930's. But the situation here is so desperate that one man would not be enough. We need four or five Hitlers in Vietnam."
> —Nguyen Cao Ky

"Frank Sinatra, I consider him a good friend."
> —Mickey Cohen

"I trust the first lion he meets will do his duty."
> —J. P. Morgan on Teddy Roosevelt's safari

"A typical triumph of modern science to find the only part of Randolph [Churchill] that was not malignant and cut it out of him."
> —Evelyn Waugh

"The reason so many people showed up at Louis B. Mayer's funeral was because they wanted to make sure he was dead."
—Samuel Goldwyn

"Adolf Hitler was the first pop star. It certainly wasn't his politics."
—David Bowie

"Paint Johnny Torrio in a corner and he'll walk off with your brush."
—Jack McPhaul, journalist

"This agreement would not have been realized without the tireless efforts and Kissinger-like negotiating brilliance of Yoko Ono Lennon."
—Allen Klein, on the settlement of eight years' dispute of Beatles finances

"He'd drink beer out of a policeman's boot."
—Brendan Behan

"I just got off the phone with Sonny Barger [President of the Hell's Angels]. He wants me to appear as a character witness for him at his murder trial and said he'd be glad to appear as a character witness on my behalf if I ever needed one. Needless to say, I readily agreed."
—Thomas King Forcade, publisher of *High Times*

"Moe Dalitz is a respected citizen."
—Jimmy Hoffa

"Well, it's probably better to have him inside the tent pissing out than outside the tent pissing in."
—Lyndon B. Johnson, on not firing J. Edgar Hoover

"They're giving bank robbing a bad name."
> —John Dillinger, on Bonnie and Clyde

"Songs were made on him, extolling his kindness."
> —Captain Bligh on himself

"She has a double chin and an overdeveloped chest. So I can hardly describe her as the most beautiful creature I've ever seen."
> —Richard Burton, on Elizabeth Taylor

"Doctor Strangelove wouldn't have lasted three weeks in the Pentagon."
> —Herman Kahn

"Nobody shoots at Santa Claus."
> —Al Smith

"Yay, Al!"
> —Boy Scouts, cheering for Al Capone, supplier of free tickets to Evanston Dyce Stadium

Motoring Tips

"**F**antastic, fantastic. That'd be a real man's car. Can you just imagine the looks on people's faces when you roll up somewhere in a Nazi staff car?"
>—Anita Pallenberg, on Keith Richards' Mercedes

"The sedan represents the wife, the convertible represents the mistress."
>—Doctor Dichter, father of motivational research

"Old Cadillacs never die."
>—Dizzy Gillespie

"I never drive over 50 kmph in densely populated areas."
>—Adolf Hitler

"Some people say a front-engine car handles best. Some people say a rear-engine car handles best. I say a rented car handles best."
>—P. J. O'Rourke

No Kidding

"Class, that's the only thing that counts in life. Class. Without class and style a man's a bum, he might as well be dead."
—Bugsy Siegel

"There is flogging with style and flogging without style."
—President Zia ul-Haq, of Pakistan

"The Führer is always right."
—Joachim von Ribbentrop

"Laws are made to be broken."
—John Wilson, English author

"Treaties are like piecrust. They are made to be broken."
—Lenin

"In the future, there will be fewer but better Russians."
—Joseph Stalin

"The chief problem of lower-income farmers is poverty."
—Nelson Rockefeller

"Tough times make monkeys eat red peppers."
—Frank Costello

"You can get much further with a kind word and a gun than you can with a kind word alone."
—Al Capone

"The tragic lesson of guilty men walking around free in this country has not been lost on the criminal community."
—Richard Nixon

"Knowledge is ruin to my young men." -
—Adolf Hitler

"They will only cause the lower classes to move about needlessly."
—The Duke of Wellington, on early steam railroads

"Vito wants everything to be legal."
—Joe Valachi, on Vito Genovese's predilection for justifying murders to his peers before committing them

"Whenever businessmen gather together it is to plot against the public interest."
—Adam Smith

"Once the toothpaste is out of the tube, it's hard to get it back in."
—H. R. (Bob) Haldeman

"In this business, you can't win 'em all."
>—Johnny Roselli, negotiator
>of JFK-Mafia "contract" on
>Fidel Castro

"The only good Indians I ever saw were dead."
>—General Philip Sheridan

"The wise and intelligent are coming belatedly to realize that alcohol, and not the dog, is man's best friend. Rover is taking a beating—and he should."
>—W. C. Fields

"Mothers and Dads that take their children to church never get into trouble."
>—J. Edgar Hoover

"You should not interpret by my use of 'least unlikely' that ultimately, or of when the final decision is made, that that may not be the decision, but what I am saying is that it is only one of the matters under consideration and decision has not been made."
>—Richard Nixon

"Death is psychosomatic."
>—Charles Manson

"At the risk of being accused of fruity tendencies, I must insist that, as a work of straight art, the well-muscled male figure is far superior to that of the blubbery looking female."
>—George Lincoln Rockwell

"Nice guys finish last."
>—Leo Durocher

"We say that cats are playful creatures, perhaps they say the same about us."
—Adolf Hitler

"A tree's a tree . . . how many more do you need to look at?"
—Ronald Reagan

"You have to be a bastard to make it, and that's a fact. And the Beatles are the biggest bastards on earth."
—John Lennon

"A single death is a tragedy, a million deaths is a statistic."
—Joseph Stalin

"You live by the gun and the knife, and die by the gun and the knife."
—Joe Valachi

"The time may have come when the issue of race could benefit from a period of 'benign neglect.' "
—Daniel Patrick Moynihan

"The hardest thing in the world to find is an honest partner in a skin game."
—Arnold Rothstein

"A long neck is good only for hanging!"
—Tsar Peter III

"We only kill each other."
—Bugsy Siegel

"You don't walk out of the Stones. They carry you out."

—Keith Richards

"I wouldn't believe Hitler was dead, even if he told me so himself."

—Hjalmar Schact, Nazi Economics Minister

Dear Warden

"**F**irst thing we do, let's kill all the lawyers."
>—Shakespeare, *Henry VI*,
>Part II

"The only people I would permit to fight duels would be priests and lawyers."
>—Adolf Hitler

"No one stands closer to the criminal in mentality than the lawyer."
>—Adolf Hitler

"I don't want a lawyer to tell me what I cannot do; I hire him to tell me how to do what I want to do."
>—J. P. Morgan

"All mouthpieces are thieves."
>—Jimmy "the Weasel" Fratianno

"I need another lawyer like I need another hole in my head."
>—Jimmy "the Weasel" Fratianno

"Don't you like me, Mr. Moran?"
"I like you, Your Honor . . . but I am suspicious of you."
>—George "Bugs" Moran

"A lawyer with a briefcase can steal more than a hundred men with guns."

—Mario Puzo

"Everyone else gets arrested by a cop. I got to get arrested by a disciple of Freud."

—Fred W. Demara, "The Great Impostor"

"They are nothing but precinct captains in long robes."

—Al Capone, on the Supreme Court

"You buy a judge by weight, like iron in a junk yard. A justice of the peace or a magistrate can be had for a five-dollar bill. In the municipal courts he will cost you ten. In the circuit or the superior courts he wants fifteen. The state appellate courts or the State Supreme Court is on a par with the Federal courts. By the time a judge reaches such courts he is middle-aged, thick around the middle, fat between the ears. He's heavy. You can't buy a Federal judge for less than a twenty-dollar bill."

—Jake "Greasy Thumb" Guzik

"Nobody takes a bribe. Of course at Christmas if you happen to hold out your hat and somebody happens to put a little something in it, well, that's different."

—New York City Police Commissioner (Ret.) William P. O'Brien, instructions to the force

"You subpoena me and you're going to get a big
fat fucking surprise."

> —Frank Sinatra, to Edward
> Olsen, then Chairman, Nevada
> State Gaming Board

"If a policeman detains you, even for a moment,
against your will, you are not guilty of murder but
only manslaughter. If the policeman uses force of
arms, you may kill him in self-defense and emerge
from the law unscathed."

> —Michael J. Ahearn, attorney
> to Al Capone

"Overpaid dumb bastards, they couldn't spring a
pickpocket."

> —Al Capone, on his lawyers

"Gentlemen, as you have been unable to obtain
proof of any of my numerous crimes, you have
been reduced to condemning me for the only one I
have never committed."

> —Don Vito Cascio Ferro, Ma-
> fia Boss of Bosses, after be-
> ing convicted on trumped-up
> charges of smuggling

"I can't see that it's wrong to give him a little legal experience before he goes out to practice law."

> —John F. Kennedy, on ap-
> pointing Robert Kennedy At-
> torney General

"When I came back to Dublin I was courtmar-
tialed in my absence and sentenced to death in my
absence, so I said they could shoot me in my absence."

> —Brendan Behan

"Mr. Druggen isn't in today.
"Mr. Lake also had an appointment downtown.
They'll be back after dinner."

> —Prison warden, to reporter
> who came to jail to interview
> gangsters Frank Lane and
> Terry Druggen

"In all my years of public life I have never ob-
structed justice."

> —Richard Nixon

"I absolutely refuse to accept either a pardon or
a commutation should either one or the other be
offered me."

> —Carl Panzram, mass mur-
> derer

"I won't cause you any trouble except to es-
cape."

> —John Dillinger

"I own the police."

> —Al Capone

"Having a judge on your side can't hurt you—in
fact, it's worth paying for. Just be thankful you
don't have to buy the jury."

> —Ray Schultz, journalist

That's All She Wrote (Famous Last Words)

"There are many of us in this old world of ours who hold that things break about even for all of us. I have observed, for example, that we all get about the same amount of ice. The rich get it in the summer and the poor get it in the winter."

—Bat Masterson

"Give my love to mother."

—Francis "Two Gun" Crowley, Prohibition gunman

"I want to wipe off the chair after that rat sat in it."

—Francis "Two Gun" Crowley (his next-to-last words)

"I came here to die, not make a speech."

—Crawford "Cherokee Bill" Goldsby

"These are the last two friends I have."

—Lord Northcliffe, referring to his Bible and his revolver

"Oh well, maybe they have guitars and bitchin' cars in Heaven."

> —Charles Schmid, "the Tucson Murderer," on being sentenced to death

"I'm here on a framed-up case."

> —Louis "Lepke" Buchalter, President of Murder, Inc.

"Oh, oh, dog biscuits and when he is happy, he doesn't get snappy . . . Mother is the best bet and don't let Satan draw you too fast . . . French-Canadian bean soup. I want to pay. Let them leave me alone."

> —Dutch Schultz

"I've had eighteen straight whiskies. I think it is a record."

> —Dylan Thomas

"I am Heinrich Himmler."

> —Heinrich Himmler

"I ain't no copper."

> —Frank Gusenberg, victim of the Saint Valentine's Day Massacre

"Take no prisoners!"

> —General George Armstrong Custer

"Ah, gentlemen, if I had been able to read and write I could have exterminated the human race."

> —Michele Caruso, Sicilian bandit, died 1863

So Long, Suckers

"**H**ello, suckers."

> Texas Guinan, Prohibition hostess

"Never give a sucker an even break, or smarten up a chump."

> —W. C. Fields

"People who want something for nothing are life's suckers."

> —Meyer Lanksy

"There's a sucker born every minute."

> —P. T. Barnum

"In the postwar years, there were two born every minute."

> —P. J. O'Rourke

The Usual Suspects

(The following were not arraigned in time for sentencing elsewhere in this book.)

"All journalists are spies. I know. I have been one."

> —President Mobutu Sese Seku, of Zaire

"Immature artists imitate. Mature artists steal."
> —Pablo Picasso

"If the facts don't fit the theory, change the facts."
> —Albert Einstein

"I suppose there ain't no wars around so they had to put me on the front page."
> —Dutch Schultz

"When I hear the word culture, I reach for my revolver."

> —Hermann Göring

"Perhaps he didn't want to commit himself."
> —Tammany aide, explaining why Boss Charley Murphy didn't join the crowd in the singing of the National Anthem

"I now know how Tojo felt when he was planning Pearl Harbor."

>—Robert F. Kennedy, to JFK during the Cuban Missile Crisis, when destruction of the missile sites was being considered

"There is no need for propaganda to be rich in intellectual content."

>—Joseph Goebbels

"I'm not smart enough to lie."

>—Ronald Reagan

"If you can't convince 'em, confuse 'em."

>—Harry Truman

"Give the investigators an hors d'ouevre and maybe they won't come back for the main course."

>—Richard Nixon

"So I lied. So what?"

>—Thomas King Forcade

"Who's that fat Jap?"

>—Spiro T. Agnew

"Anybody goes into business, they ought to start their own union."

>—Joey Gallo

"Bullets, like wine, come in vintages. Mexican '55 is a good year. '52, not so good."

>—Fidel Castro

"Steal from one person and it's plagiarism; steal from four people and it's scholarship."

>—Wilson Mizner

"We're going to sell the Eiffel Tower again."
"We can't do that. We don't own it any more. We already sold it."

> —"Count" Victor Lustig and "Dapper Dan" Collins, con game partners, in conversation

"I promise you I'll never bribe another juror."

> —William J. Fallon, after his acquittal for jury tampering

"The dictatorship of the Communist party is maintained by recourse to every form of violence."

> —Leon Trotsky

"You've lost your job,
You've lost your dough,
Your jewels and handsome houses,
But things could be worse, you know,
You haven't lost your trousers."

> —comic valentine left on the body of "Machine Gun Jack" McGurn

"Goodness had nothing to do with it."

> —Mae West

"They'll have to shoot me first to take my gun."

> —Roy Rogers

"Everybody should rise up and say, 'Thank you, Mr. President, for bombing Haiphong.'"

> —Martha Mitchell

"Let the worthy citizens of Chicago get their liquor the best way they can. I'm sick of the job. It's a thankless one and full of grief."
—Al Capone

Acknowledgments

The Bad Guys' Quote Book could not have been compiled without the diligent research of Charles Rehwinkel, curator of the Warren Street Museum and America's leading expert on totalitarian visual phenomena.

Additional thanks are due to Ed Dwyer, Douglas Ward Kelley, Trina Robbins, Michael Chance, Nancy Borman, Jill Seiden, Joe Schenkman, Alexander Grant, Neville Gerson, and Yossarian. For special insights I am forever indebted to Toby Mamis, Ted Mann, Jules Siegel, and Melvin B. Shestack.

Finally, I would like to thank my beautiful wife, Kathy, for her help, support, and love.

RS

Coming soon from AVON

The Bad Guys' Quote Book Volume Two!

Our researchers and editors are hard at work on the second volume of the Bad Guys' Quote Book, which will incorporate the most memorable sayings of Joe McCarthy, Howard Hughes, Muammar al-Khadafy, Yassir Arafat, Captain Kidd, "Bob" Vesco, Attilla the Hun, and many, many more—as soon as we can find them. If you can help us out with any suggestions, information, quotations, corrections and other additions, please send them to:

Bad Guys' Quote Book Volume Two
Avon Books
1790 Broadway
New York, N.Y. 10019

You'll have a great time explaining to your lawyer why you did. Thanks!

THE CONCISE COLUMBIA ENCYCLOPEDIA

THE COLUMBIA UNIVERSITY PRESS

A new, comprehensive, and authoritative, one-volume encyclopedia of biographies, facts and information for everyday
use in the 80's. Written under the guidance of a distinguished
panel of scholars in every field, THE CONCISE COLUMBIA
ENCYCLOPEDIA is the product of years of careful research
and planning to make an encyclopedia's worth of information
available in one volume which is small enough to take
anywhere!

- Over 15,000 entries covering every field of information
- Over 3,000 articles on up-to-date scientific and technical
  subjects—from computers to robotics and quarks
- Broad coverage of people and topics of contemporary
  importance—from Sandra Day O'Connor and Luciano
  Pavarotti to genetic engineering and herpes simplex
- Over 5,000 biographies of notable men and women, past
  and present
- Illustrations, diagrams, charts, national and regional maps
- A 16-page world atlas of political and topographical maps
- Over 50,000 cross references to additional information
- Pronunciation guide for difficult names and words
- Metric equivalents for all measurements
- Plus special tables listing U.S. presidents, Supreme Court
  justices, popes, prime ministers, rulers, royal dynasties,
  national parks, theaters, orchestras, languages, planets,
  elements—and much more!

An AVON Trade Paperback   63396-5/$14.95

Available wherever paperbacks are sold or directly from the publisher. Include $1.00 per
copy for postage and handling; allow 6-8 weeks for delivery. Avon Books, Dept BP, Box 767,
Rte 2, Dresden, TN 38225.

Con Col En 7-83